D0715334

JOE SHUSTER

LOBO CREATED BY
ROGER SLIFER AND
...FFEN

520 391 39 7

www.raintreepublishers.co.uk
Visit our website to find out
more information about
Raintree books.

To order:
☎ Phone 0845 6044371
📄 Fax +44 (0) 1865 312263
✉ Email myorders@raintreepublishers.co.uk

Customers from outside the UK please telephone +44 1865 312262

Raintree is an imprint of Capstone Global Library Limited,
a company incorporated in England and Wales having its
registered office at 7 Pilgrim Street, London, EC4V 6LB –
Registered company number: 6695582

First published by Stone Arch Books in 2011
First published in hardback and paperback
in the United Kingdom by Capstone Global Library in 2011
The moral rights of the proprietor have been asserted.

Art Director: Bob Lentz
Designer: Hilary Wacholz
Production Specialist: Michelle Biedscheid
Editor: Vaarunika Dharmapala
Originated by Capstone Global Library Ltd
Printed and bound in China by Leo Paper Products Ltd

ISBN 978 1 406 22529 7 (hardback)
15 14 13 12 11
10 9 8 7 6 5 4 3 2 1

ISBN 978 1 406 22534 1 (paperback)
15 14 13 12 11
10 9 8 7 6 5 4 3 2

British Library Cataloguing in Publication Data
A full catalogue record for this book is
available from the British Library.

CONTENTS

CHAPTER 1

THE BOUNTY HUNTER

On the faraway planet of Apokolips, a spaceship rumbled to a halt, kicking up a cloud of dirt on the landing pad. When the dust cleared, a door in the ship's side slid open. Out stepped Lobo, the universe's most ruthless bounty hunter. He was tall and muscular. He wore biker boots and a black leather jacket. Over one shoulder, he cradled a crowbar.

Behind Lobo, a troop of Apokolips soldiers stumbled out of the spaceship. Some of them wore bandages around their heads. Others had arms in slings.

Next to the landing pad was a walkway. It led to a menacing looking castle in the distance. Lobo's lengthy strides quickly carried him to the castle's front door. The alien soldiers followed.

With a swing of his crowbar, Lobo bashed the door down. **KRAK!** He then kicked through its splintered remains and strode down a wide corridor.

THUD! THUD! His boots stomped loudly on the stone floor. The soldiers trembled behind him.

At the end of the corridor, large brass doors swung inwards, revealing the castle's throne room.

"Come in," a deep voice boomed from within.

Lobo advanced, and the Apokolips soldiers poured into the room after him.

On the opposite side of the throne room sat Darkseid, ruler of Apokolips. To his right stood his son, the ogre-like Kalibak. On his left was the evil scientist Desaad.

"Thank you for coming," Darkseid said to Lobo. "I hope my minions didn't bother you."

The soldiers now formed a half circle around Lobo.

"They *did* interrupt my nap," Lobo snarled. "So I had to break a few arms for them."

Several of the bandaged aliens shuddered as Lobo shifted his crowbar from one shoulder to the other.

"I wouldn't have asked you here if it wasn't important," Darkseid said.

"What could be more important than my beauty sleep?" Lobo said, standing proudly in front of Apokolips' ruler. "It's not easy looking this good."

Darkseid stood up and walked over to Lobo, placing a hand on the bounty hunter's shoulder. "Have you heard of Superman?" he asked.

"Yeah, we've tangled a time or two," Lobo replied. "What do you want with him?"

"Come this way," Darkseid said.

He led Lobo behind his throne. "Superman's been quite bothersome. He's always in the way of my plans to conquer Earth," Darkseid explained.

"And I need something to be done about that," he continued.

"What do you expect little old me to do to Superman?" Lobo asked.

The pair stopped walking. They now stood behind the throne.

"Your job," Darkseid said. "You're a bounty hunter after all."

"Hey, even though he wears tights and a cape, Superman's no pushover," Lobo said. "It's going to cost you some serious cash if you're asking me to take him on."

"Will this be enough to hire your services?" Darkseid asked, motioning to the wall next to them. **CLANK! CHING!** A door burst open, and a pile of jewels, gems, and trinkets spilled on to the floor.

Lobo rushed over to the loot. Kneeling down on the floor, he grabbed two fists full of treasure and raised them above his head.

"Man, with this, I could buy new chrome headers for my bike!" Lobo exclaimed. "And I'd still have enough for that beach house near Alpha Centauri. I could probably even get front-row seats at next year's asteroid smash-up derby or ..."

While Lobo dreamt of what he would do with his reward, Desaad walked up to Darkseid and placed a long, cylindrical object in his hand. Raising the object above his head, Darkseid flicked a switch. **CLICK!** The object emitted a chain of crackling and sizzling energy. With a flick of his wrist, Darkseid snapped the chain at Lobo. It wrapped around the bounty hunter, trapping him.

"Owwww!" Lobo shouted. "What gives?"

"It's a gift," Darkseid explained. "It was designed by my scientist, Desaad. It will help you to capture Superman."

CLICK! Darkseid flicked the switch off, and the chain of energy disappeared. He then tossed the weapon to Lobo, who caught it with an outstretched hand.

"Cool! It's like my birthday, only better," Lobo chuckled. "I don't have to blow out some stupid candles to get my wish – a chance to put one over that super do-gooder."

"Do you need help reaching Earth?" Darkseid asked.

"Nah, I've got my own ride," Lobo replied.

Lobo whistled loudly. In the distance, a thunderous roar was heard. A motorcycle rumbled into the throne room, scattering the soldiers in its path. Lobo hopped on and revved its engine.

VROOOOOM! VROOOOOM!

"Next time I see you, you'll have a date with Superman," Lobo shouted as he roared off.

After the bounty hunter left, Desaad and Kalibak walked up to Darkseid. "I don't like him," Kalibak said with a grumble.

"He doesn't seem trustworthy," added Desaad.

"All that matters," Darkseid began, "is that Lobo weakens Superman enough for our plan to work."

The three of them smiled wickedly.

CHAPTER 2

TO THE RESCUE!

In the newsroom of the Daily Planet Building, Lois Lane stormed over to the desk of fellow reporter Clark Kent.

"Clark," she said, waving a copy of the *Daily Planet* newspaper in front of Clark's face. "How is it that some country bumpkin from Smallville can beat me to one of Metropolis' juiciest stories?"

On the front page of the newspaper, the headline read "Superman Saves Shock Jock Leslie Willis, by Clark Kent."

"Lucky, I guess," Clark replied with a smile.

FLAP! Lois tossed the paper down on Clark's desk. "Luck!" Lois shouted. "I was reporting the news in this city while you were still out milking cows, and that's your explanation?"

"Maybe I just have a heightened sense for news," Clark added.

"Ooooh," Lois fumed, and then stomped off.

Out of the corner of his eye, Clark saw Jimmy Olsen, a young staff photographer. He was chuckling about the exchange between Lois and Clark.

"Better not get on her bad side today, Jimmy," Clark warned, "or she'll drag you all round town looking for a story."

"I know, I know," Jimmy said. "It's just funny seeing how upset she gets when she doesn't get the front page story."

Jimmy glanced down. "So, what are you working on, Clark?" he asked.

"An interview I did with Superman," replied Clark.

"Cool, can I read it when you've finished?" asked Jimmy.

"Sure," Clark said. He turned back to his work, typing up the story on Superman.

Unknown to Lois and Jimmy, Clark had a secret identity. He was Superman, Last Son of Krypton. The rays from Earth's yellow sun gave him superpowers, such as superhuman strength, the ability to fly, and super-hearing.

A short time later, he stopped typing.

Clark tilted his head to one side. Over the clicks of his keyboard, he thought he had heard a cry for help. He waited.

"HELP!" There it was again, off in the distance. Clark leapt from his desk and headed for the exit.

"Hey, where are you going?" Lois yelled after him. "You'd better not be chasing some new story."

"No, no," Clark yelled, darting out of the door. "I spilled coffee on my shirt and need to go home to get a change of clothes."

Once outside, Clark quickly ducked into a deserted alley. Making sure no one was watching him, he shed his shirt and tie, revealing a blue uniform with a red "S" emblazoned on the chest. Superman then leapt into the air and flew away.

In the distance, he saw a bridge swaying back and forth. Cars and trucks skidded across the pavement and crashed into the guardrails. The people inside the vehicles screamed in fright. Then one car skidded off the bridge, falling towards the river far below.

Superman quickly swooped down under the car, catching it before it splashed into the water.

As he placed the car safely on the shore, Superman looked up at the teetering bridge. Any minute, another car could come tumbling from its heights. He could not stop them all.

"I knew it," a voice chuckled behind Superman. "All I needed to do was cause a little trouble, and you'd show up."

Superman whirled around. The alien bounty hunter Lobo was leaning against one of the bridge's supports.

"Lobo!" Superman exclaimed. "What are you doing here?"

"You don't seem happy to see me!" Lobo said.

"Not when you're putting people in harm's way," Superman scolded.

CRAAAAACK!! Lobo punched the bridge support. Distant screams were heard as the bridge shook.

A few large bricks crashed to the ground between him and Superman. Lobo picked up one of the bricks, which was about the size of a television, and tossed it up and down in the air.

"I knew that if I threatened some of these puny Earthlings," Lobo said, "you'd come running, all hero-like."

"Well, you found me," Superman said. "Now what do you want?"

Lobo caught the brick in his hand. He smiled wickedly, and his knuckles whitened. Then he laughed.

"This!" Lobo shouted.

Lobo threw the brick at Superman. It hit the Man of Steel in the chest and sent him reeling backwards. **SLAM!** Lobo then grabbed a nearby car and lifted it over his head. **SMASH!** He slammed it down on Superman. The Man of Steel fell to the ground in a cloud of dust.

"Owwww," Lobo said. "That's got to hurt."

"But I have another surprise for you," Lobo added. Superman sat there completely stunned.

From his back pocket, Lobo whipped out the weapon that Darkseid had given him. He clicked the switch. A chain of red energy, crackling and sizzling, dangled from it.

"What's that?" Superman asked, eyeing Lobo's weapon.

"Oh, just a little gift from a mutual friend," Lobo said. With a flick of his wrist, Lobo sent the chain of energy whipping out at Superman.

CHAPTER 3

ALIEN FACE-OFF

"Ahhh!" Superman moaned in pain.

Lobo released the chain of energy at Superman again. And for the second time, the powerful weapon struck the Man of Steel. **ZZAPPPPPPP!**

"Argh!" Superman yelled.

"Tickles, doesn't it?" Lobo laughed.

"You think this is funny?" said Superman.

"Yeah, kind of," Lobo replied, smiling from ear to ear.

Lobo whipped the energy chain at Superman again. This time, though, the Man of Steel was ready for the attack. He ducked under the sizzling energy blast, and then leapt at Lobo, punching him in the stomach. **THUD!**

"Ummmpf!" Lobo grunted as he fell.

The pair rolled to the ground, fists flying and feet kicking. While Superman and Lobo fought, a car drove up and skidded to a stop near them. **SKREEE-EEE-EEECH!** Out jumped Lois and Jimmy Olsen.

"Quick, Jimmy," Lois shouted. "Snap a couple pictures of them fighting. This is definitely worth a front-page story!"

FLASH! FLASH! Jimmy started clicking away with his camera while Lois scribbled down notes.

Suddenly, Superman slammed Lobo down on the ground with a thud, pinning him. Lobo's weapon flew out of his hand and high into the air. It landed at Lois' feet, with the chain of energy still crackling behind. **FZZZT! FZZZT!** Sparks were flying everywhere.

Lois reached down to pick up the weapon.

"Lois, be careful!" Superman shouted. He was worried she would get hurt.

While Superman was distracted, Lobo struck him square in the jaw. **POW!** The Man of Steel went sailing through the air and crashed to the ground. **THUD!**

Lobo then walked over to Lois. "I'll take that," he said. Lobo snatched the weapon from her.

Lobo spun around to face Superman, who was struggling to his feet.

"Fun time is over," Lobo snarled. "I have a job to do."

He raised the chain of energy above his head. It crackled. Then Lobo aimed the weapon at Superman, and the beam wrapped tightly around the Man of Steel.

Superman groaned and cried out in pain. He struggled with all his might to break free. Sparks shot out from the energy chain in all directions and seared everything they touched. Smoke filled the air. Then finally, after several minutes, Superman sank to his knees, exhausted.

"Ha!" Lobo laughed. "I didn't think Darkseid's toy would be able to hold you."

Just then, Lois ran over to Lobo. She repeatedly slammed her fists into his chest. "You let him go!" she yelled. "Let him go!"

Lobo reach down with his free hand and lifted Lois off the ground. She continued to hit and kick him, screaming loudly.

"Whoa, miss," Lobo laughed. "You seem to have quite the temper. Maybe you need to cool off in the river over there."

"But that's more than a hundred metres away!" Jimmy shouted.

"I bet you Superman's boots I can toss her that far," Lobo bragged.

"No, no!" Jimmy shouted.

Lobo steadied himself then gave a mighty heave.

AAAAAHHH! Lois screamed as she sailed through the air.

Superman stood up, looking angry.

"Uh-oh, did that make Mr Goody Two-Shoes mad?" Lobo said, grinning.

Straining his muscles as hard as he could, Superman fought to break free of the chain of energy that was binding him. Lobo's weapon began to whir and spark. Then it burst into flames and blew up in Lobo's hand.

ZHHINNGG!

"Ow!" Lobo exclaimed.

As Lobo was holding his sore hand, Superman was off in a flash, flying after Lois. He caught her just as she was about splash into the middle of the river.

"Thanks, Superman," she said, hugging the Man of Steel.

"Now, it's time to stop Lobo," Superman said, setting Lois down on the bank of the river, "before someone gets hurt."

He was off again, zooming towards Lobo.

Superman crashed into the bounty hunter, and they rolled to the ground. After a couple of moments, Superman stood victorious, holding Lobo over his head.

Suddenly, a blue energy field surrounded both super-strong fighters.

"Is this your doing?" Superman asked, dropping Lobo to the ground with a heavy thud.

"Nah," Lobo replied. "I don't like force fields. Body bags are more my style."

CHAPTER 4

KALIBAK AND DESAAD

As Superman looked up, he saw a giant airship. The blue energy rays were coming from it.

"Darkseid ..." Superman muttered.

As soon as a door in the ship's hull whooshed open, Kalibak and Desaad stepped out of the ship. Lobo began to yell at them. "Hey, what's going on!" he shouted. "This wasn't part of our deal."

Lobo struck the force field. **ZZRRRRTT!** It didn't burst, just sizzled and flickered.

"I should have known you were behind Lobo's new toy, Desaad," Superman said.

"It seems you worked that out a little late, Superman," Desaad replied as he inspected the force field around Superman and Lobo.

Turning to Kalibak, he added, "The force field is secure. Now we'll have two new residents in the Apokolips dungeons instead of one."

"You dirty, rotten –" Lobo fumed. "When I get a hold of you ..."

Kalibak and Desaad walked back to the ship, laughing.

Superman struck the force field as hard as he could. A loud **SNAP!** was heard as it flickered under the might of Superman's blow, but the force field did not give.

The spaceship lifted off, floating above where Superman and Lobo were trapped. Then a large steel cable lowered down, and pulled the force field inside the ship. The hull doors closed. Now, they were surrounded by electronics, and all sorts of strange devices.

Superman leant into the force field with all his strength. It snapped and fizzled, but it still didn't budge.

"Hey, Mr Blue Tights," Lobo mocked Superman. "If I couldn't bust through that force field, there's little chance you can do it."

"Shhh," Superman said.

As he continued to push, Superman heard something. From the corner of the ship, he heard a high-pitched sound.

The harder he pushed, the louder it got.

Superman turned to Lobo. "Quick," he said. "What did they hire you to do?"

"To bring you back to Apokolips," Lobo replied.

"And that weapon?" Superman asked.

"I was told it would help capture you," Lobo said.

"See that box on the wall over there?" Superman said to Lobo. "That controls the force field."

"Yeah, so?" Lobo snorted.

"Desaad created this force field to capture me," Superman said. "They didn't plan on you being in here, too."

"What's your point, Superman?" growled Lobo.

"Well, if the two of us work together," Superman explained, "we may be able to drain the controller of its power and break free."

As they were talking, the ship shot upwards. It flew even higher into the sky.

"We'd better hurry," Superman yelled over the sound of the rushing wind. "Soon they'll enter a boom tube, which will take us all to Apokolips. We may never escape."

"Hey, if this gives me a chance to knock Kalibak and Desaad's heads together," Lobo said, "then I'll give it a try."

Lobo pounded on the wall of the force field. It crackled under the pressure of his fist, but did not seem to weaken.

But Superman knew the high-pitched whining sound was getting louder.

Superman leant into the wall of the force field, opposite Lobo. He pushed with all his strength while Lobo smashed the force field with his fist. The controller began to squeal loudly and smoke.

"Just a little more," Superman shouted.

Suddenly, the controller exploded!

CHAPTER 5

SWEET JUSTICE

As Kalibak was sitting at the ship's controls, a loud noise startled him. **BANG!**

"What was that?" Kalibak asked.

He pointed to the rear of the ship's control room. A large dent had been made in the metal wall behind them.

"How –?" Kalibak began, but before he could finish, the sound of breaking metal interrupted him.

The metal wall split open, and Lobo's grinning mug poked through the gaping hole.

"You two are in for some pain," Lobo said with a smile.

Kalibak and Desaad stared back at him in silent fear.

*　　*　　*

Much later, Lobo zoomed down towards the surface of Apokolips. He was riding his motorcycle. Kalibak and Desaad, looking bruised and battered, were tied to the back of his bike.

Instead of stopping at the landing pad, Lobo cruised towards the castle, leaving a trail of dust behind him. He drove through the castle door, down the corridor, and into the throne room.

Lobo skidded to a halt in front of Darkseid's throne.

"Where's Superman?" Darkseid asked as Lobo leapt off his bike. "Oh, he got away," Lobo replied. "Then you won't get paid," Darkseid said, scowling.

"Well, I would have captured him," Lobo said as he pulled Kalibak and Desaad off the back of his bike and dropped them at Darkseid's feet. "Only these two goons got in my way."

Lobo folded his arms. "So, how about you pay me for bringing them back in one piece."

Darkseid glared disapprovingly at his son and the evil scientist. "Fine, fine," he said to Lobo, with a dismissive wave. "Take whatever you can carry."

Lobo grinned and pulled a large black sack out of his back pocket.

*   *   *

In the newsroom of the *Daily Planet*, Clark Kent typed away at his desk. Jimmy Olsen approached with a copy of that day's paper. On the front page was a picture of Lobo holding Lois off the ground while she kicked and screamed. The headline read "Local Reporter Battles Cosmic Biker," with the byline "by Clark Kent."

"Great photo, Jimmy," Clark said.

"Thanks, Clark," Jimmy blushed. "But, I don't get it. How did you get this story? I didn't even see you there."

"I've been working on that interview with Superman," Clark explained. "So he gave me the scoop."

"You must have a pretty good relationship with him," Jimmy said.

"You could say that," Clark replied with a grin.

As they were talking, Perry White rushed into the room. Hot on his trail was Lois Lane.

She was waving a copy of the *Daily Planet* newspaper in front of him. "How could you bump my story to page two?" she demanded.

"It was an editorial choice," Mr White replied. "Our readers like celebrity news, and you, Lois, happen to be a celebrity."

"But people were in danger. A bridge could have collapsed," Lois explained. "This is just a, just a –"

"Face it, Lois," Mr White interrupted. "You'd rather have your story on the front page than your picture."

Mr White stormed into his office, slamming the door shut behind him before Lois could follow.

Lois stood there dumbfounded for a second. Then she scanned the newsroom. Seeing Clark at his desk, she stormed over to him.

"You stole my scoop!" Lois scolded. "How did you get to this story first, Mr Smallville?"

"Well, Lois," Clark said, leaning back in his chair and smiling, "I'm afraid that's between me and the Man of Steel himself."

FROM THE DESK OF CLARK KENT

WHO IS LOBO?

Lobo is known as the most successful bounty hunter in the entire universe. He always gets his man, even if it means destroying entire planets in pursuit of his prey. In fact, Lobo loves breaking things – and people – so the line of work suits him well. Despite being a self-proclaimed "bad man", Lobo is always true to his word. He will never break a promise, but he does tend to *bend* them quite often. His employers must choose their words carefully, or they will end up in a deal they had not bargained for.

- Lobo is the last member of his race, the Czarnians, because he destroyed his own home planet in a fit of rage!

- Lobo zooms around from planet to planet on his trusty, customized motorcycle, the Hog. Since Lobo does not need to breathe, he can undergo interstellar travel at super-speed without even wearing a space suit.

- Lobo's accelerated healing abilities allow him to regenerate lost limbs with great speed. In fact, Lobo can heal from any injury if he is given enough time.

- Despite his own bad body odour, Lobo has an amazing sense of smell. He is able to sniff out his prey from as far as a galaxy away! He also has the tracking skills of an expert hunter, so hiding from the Main Man is nearly impossible.

- Lobo has a variety of high-tech weaponry, including a titanium chain with a hook on its end, frag grenades, and giant carving blades. However, being the blunt instrument that he is, Lobo usually prefers to use a crowbar in combat.

BIOGRAPHIES

Blake A. Hoena has a Masters of Fine Arts in Creative Writing. Since graduating, Blake has written more than thirty books for children, including *Harley Quinn's Shocking Surprise*, *Poison Ivy's Deadly Garden*, *Under the Red Sun*, and *Livewire!*

Rick Burchett has worked as a comics artist for over 25 years. He has received the comics industry's Eisner Award three times, the Haxtur Award once, and has been nominated for the Eagle Award.

Lee Loughridge has been working in comics for more than fifteen years. He currently lives in a tent on the beach.

GLOSSARY

conquer overcome and take control of something

dumbfounded to be so amazed or shocked that you cannot speak

emit release heat, light, or sound

inspect look at something very carefully

menacing dangerous

minion servant of a person in power

ruthless cruel and without pity

scoop story that is published or broadcast before anyone else reports it

DISCUSSION QUESTIONS

1. Is Lobo a super-villain, a super hero, or something else? Why?

2. If you could have the powers of any character in this book, which would you choose? Discuss your answers.

3. This book has ten illustrations. Which one is your favourite? Why?

WRITING PROMPTS

1. Imagine you have just completed a very difficult bounty hunt. But instead of gold and jewels, Darkseid has offered you anything you desire. What rewards would you choose? Write about it.

2. Write another chapter to this story. What does Lobo spend his hard-earned money on? Does Superman come after him? You decide!

3. Lobo cruises across galaxies on his customized Hog motorcycle. Create your own space vehicle, writing about its features and cool touches. Then draw a picture of your new ride.

MORE NEW SUPERMAN ADVENTURES!

LAST SON OF KRYPTON

THE MUSEUM MONSTERS

THE STOLEN SUPERPOWERS

LIVEWIRE!

THE MENACE OF METALLO